REVENGE

VICTORIA KOMAR

PAGE PUBLISHING, INC.
Conneaut Lake, PA

First originally published by Page Publishing 2021

ISBN 978-1-6624-1889-1 (pbk)
ISBN 978-1-6624-1888-4 (digital)

Printed in the United States of America

JOHN WAS SITTING at his desk in black pants with food stains on them and was wearing a blue-striped shirt that wouldn't entirely stay tucked in because his pants were a little loose. At the office, he was looking at a case file that had chocolate stains on it when Matt walked in with a steaming cup of coffee in his hand. Matt had an army-style haircut, was wearing black sunglasses, and a well-pressed red dress shirt.

"John," said Matt.

Looking up from his file, John said, "What's up?"

"Nothing much, grabbed some coffee. What are you looking at?"

Looking up, he said, "It's nothing. Don't worry about it."

Matt went and grabbed the file from his hands and said, "Let me see."

While trying to grab it back, John said, "Give it!"

Looking at it, Matt said, "Dave Smith? Who's that?"

Grabbing the file back, John said, "Nobody. Don't worry about it."

"Wait, is that the file you've been looking at for the past week now?"

"Does it matter?"

"A little. What makes that so important that your eyes have been glued to it?"

"Back in high school, he went to jail because of me, and he said he would kill me when he gets out."

"A lot of people say that, and they never follow through with it. What makes him so special?"

"I got a phone call last week from a number I didn't recognize, so naturally, I sent it to voicemail. When I listened to it later, it was Dave. Dave said he had been out of jail for some time now, and he didn't forget what he told me in high school. He said he is going to kill me, so I'm going to try and stop him first."

"What does this have to do with the file though?"

"It says here that he has been selling drugs in different alleys, but he never gets caught. He moves them before anyone gets there. I figured if I can catch him selling them, I can lock him back up."

"Didn't sending him to jail start this whole thing?"

"Yes, but I have the power to do something about it now."

"Doesn't mean he won't kill you."

"You aren't helping. I'll figure this out on my own."

"Don't get your panties in a knot. I'll help you."

We both grabbed our things and went to the car. We headed to an alley where there was suspicion of Dave being seen. We walked through the alley that was covered in water and mud and saw nothing but rats and old boxes.

"Okay, so what's next?" said Matt.

"I don't know. There are barely any clues in this file. It only says where he has been seen, but no one has found anything at those places, so we have nothing."

"Well, why don't you start by telling me what happened in high school."

"Why?"

"Maybe something from the past could help us with this case."

"All right. Back in high school, I was the shy band kid who would sit in the corner of the classroom doing the assignments and reading over my music sheets. I didn't have many friends, which is why I would walk to class alone and eat by myself during lunch. Dave was one of the popular kids. He was average built, would always wear a sweatshirt no matter the weather, and when he gave you that look, you knew you were in for it. He liked picking on people who were smaller than he was. You would go to him if you wanted answers for a test or to buy drugs. For most of the year, I was his punching bag. He would shove me into lockers and trip me in the hallway. I was afraid to say no to him, so I would do what he told me to do. One time, he needed answers for a bio test, and he didn't want to get caught stealing them, so he made me go and get them for him. I ended up getting suspended for that because I wouldn't rat him out. He knew I was afraid of him, so he figured he could use my locker to store his drugs. Half the time he wouldn't even tell me they were there, so when I would get my books, a bag of them would fall out of my locker, and I would have to put them back before a teacher saw. At one point, the teachers did locker checks. They found drugs inside some of the kids' lockers, but not mine. Dave took them out right before the teacher looked in there."

Matt interrupted, saying, "See, he didn't want you to get in trouble."

"No, he didn't want to lose his drugs. Now let me continue my story. After a while, I was getting annoyed and didn't want to be a part of this anymore. I didn't want to get in trouble for things Dave was doing. I tried saying something to him, but he took me behind the school, roughed me up a bit, and told me if I tried backing out again, I would have more than a black eye and a cut-up lip."

Matt interrupted again and said, "Did you tell your parents?"

"I didn't want to get them involved. My mom would have contacted the school and would have caused a scene. My dad probably would have killed him because of anger management issues, and I didn't want him going to jail."

"So what did you tell them?"

"I told them my friends and I were playing football, and the ball hit me in the eye. When I went to catch it, I bit my lip in the process. Anyway, a few weeks later, I stayed after school to get help on an assignment from one of my teachers, and when we were done, I went to my locker to get something, and out of nowhere, a muscular guy came up to me and shoved me into my locker and said, 'Where are my drugs?' I told him I didn't know where they were, but he didn't like that answer very much. He pulled a gun out of his jacket, held it to my head, and asked again, 'Where are my drugs?' I told him that Dave had them, and before I could finish the sentence, Dave came walking down the hallway. He let me go, and I ran as far away from there as I could. I've never been so scared in my life. At that moment, I knew I didn't want Dave pushing me around anymore and that I had to do something about it. A week later, I went to the principal's office and told her that I suspected drugs in Dave's locker, and she told me that if I was wrong and if she checked his locker and there wasn't anything in there, I would get in a lot of trouble for assuming someone with no proof. I told her I knew the consequences and that I still wanted her to check. The following day, the principal, as well as an officer, went to Dave's locker and told Dave to open it, and when he did, there was a big bag of drugs sitting there. The officer arrested Dave right then and there and walked him out of the school. While he was being taken away, he told me that he knew it was me and that he would get revenge, even if it were the last thing he did. After that, I never saw him again."

"Well, that's the story. So what do we do now?"

"Let me think." After a pause, Matt said, "Do you still have Dave's number in your phone?"

"I think so. Why?"

"Because I can call him and say I want to buy some drugs, and then we can meet him and finally catch him."

"I don't know, dude."

"Look, you even said it yourself, we have no clues on this guy, and he has never been caught. If you want to find him, this is our best way, and by what you just told me, I doubt he would hesitate to kill you if he has the chance."

"All right, but we still need to be careful. Who knows what Dave is capable of nowadays?"

* * *

We headed back to the office where we made the phone call on Matt's cell. The phone rang, and Dave answered. In a tired sounding tone, Dave said, "Hello?"

In an overly happy tone, Matt said, "Hey, Dave! What's up?"

"Who's this?"

"You don't know me, but I heard from a friend, who knows a friend, who knows you, that you sell the best drugs around, and I could go for some right now, so what do you say? You selling any?"

While scratching his head, Dave said, "I don't know, man. I don't even know you, and I don't like selling to people I have never met before."

"Come on, man. I heard you were the best, and I wouldn't be calling if I had another way."

"Fine. Meet me at the abandoned building over by the Laundromat tomorrow at noon and bring $250 with you. Come alone."

"Got it. See you then."

* * *

"Abandoned building? He has never done his deals in an abandoned building before," said John.

"Maybe he wanted to switch things up. We know where he is going to be now, so tomorrow at noon, we go in and we get this guy."

"All right."

* * *

The next morning, John went to the building an hour before Matt. He wanted to deal with Dave once and for all. He waited in his car till he saw Dave go in. Once John saw him go in, he waited a few minutes and then followed behind. The building hadn't been used in some time, so it was run down. He pulled out his gun, and he slowly walked through what was once the entranceway. He looked around to see if Dave was there. He didn't see him, so he continued through the building into another room. The room was a little darker compared to the first one, so it was hard to see what was there, but he could make out some boards and other old items that were in the building. He walked a little more and saw a bag on the table. He slowly walked toward it with his guard up.

He heard a voice behind him and felt a gun on his neck. "Well, won't you look at who it is. John Bow, the private investigator."

"How did you know?" said John.

"You think I would fall for the oldest trick in the book? I knew you were a private investigator, and I knew if I left you a voicemail and did some drug deals, you would try to catch me."

"So you aren't going to kill me?"

"No, I am, but we are going to talk first. Now put your gun on the ground and slowly turn around."

He threw his gun on the ground and slowly turned around.

"You ruined my life by sending me to jail."

"Well, I wouldn't have had to if you didn't always leave your drugs in my locker."

"Save it. You couldn't handle me then, and you can't handle me now. I'm finishing this once and for all."

John was still standing in front of Dave and his gun when he cocked it back, getting ready to shoot him in the face. Before Dave hits the trigger, John grabbed a board that was on the table behind him and hit Dave's hand, knocking the gun out of it and tackled him to the ground.

Dave pushed John off and took a board that was on the ground, and hit him in the head with it. John got a gash on his forehead, and he started to get dizzy. Dave grabbed John and punched him in the gut. John fell, and Dave went for John's gun. John kicked him in the leg, and Dave dropped John's gun and fell. Seeing how arresting Dave isn't going to be an option, John was going to have to stop Dave before he killed John. John tried to grab his gun, but Dave pulled him back. John kicked him in his stomach and crawled away with the last bit of energy he had left. He finally grabbed the gun and turned toward him. Dave pointed his gun toward John and pulled the trigger. At the same time, John pointed his gun at Dave and pulled the trigger. In slow motion, John could see the bullet coming at him. John's shot hit Dave in the forehead, and he fell straight to the ground, while Dave's shot hit John in the shoulder. While John tried to get to his feet, he heard Matt rushing in. He must have heard the gunshots go off.

"John!" yelled Matt.

"I'm over here!" yelled John.

"Oh my gosh, John! You're bleeding!"

"I'm fine, Matt. Just a little banged up."

"But you're bleeding."

"Trust me, I'm fine."

"Where is Dave?"

"He is on the ground over there. I'm guessing dead."

"Oh, John, you didn't."

"I know, Matt, but I had to. If I didn't, he was going to kill me, and you were right. He wasn't going to let that chance slip by if he got it."

* * *

The next day, they went back to the office and looked over new cases.

"John," said Matt.

"Matt," said John.

"How are you feeling?"

"I've been better."

"I bet. I'm sorry about what you went through with Dave."

"Don't be. Sometimes you have to fight your own battles."

* * *

"Morning, John," said Matt.

"Morning, Matt," said John.

"What are you looking at?"

"Just some paperwork."

"What's on my desk?"

"I think a new case file. It came in this morning."

Matt opened up the file and looked at it. His jaw opened slightly, and he had a surprised look on his face.

"Um, John, you might want to take a look at this."

John walked over and took a look at the file. His face went white.

The End

ABOUT THE AUTHOR

VICTORIA KOMAR CURRENTLY resides in New Jersey with her family and her German shepherd named Sascha. She always enjoyed writing, but it was only a hobby until she decided to pursue it as her career when she went to college. She enjoys writing crime dramas, stories that include superpowers or magical abilities of some kind, as well as stories that focus around the underdog. In her free time, she enjoys collecting Funko pops, listening to music, playing with her dog, and coming up with new story ideas.

CPSIA information can be obtained
at www.ICGtesting.com
Printed in the USA
BVHW081141250621
610447BV00004B/790

9 781662 418891